CHRISTMAS LOVE RETURNS

MAIL ORDER BRIDES OF MILES GULCH

SUSANNAH CALLOWAY

PERSONAL WORD FROM THE AUTHOR

Dearest Readers,

Thank you so much for choosing one of my books. I am proud to be a part of the team of writers at Tica House Publishing who work joyfully to bring you stories of hope, faith, courage, and love. Your kind words and loving readership are deeply appreciated.

I would like to personally invite you to sign up for updates and to become part of our **Exclusive Reader Club**—it's completely Free to join! We'd love to welcome you!

Much love,

Susannah Calloway

VISIT HERE to Join our Reader's Club and to Receive Tica House Updates!

https://wesrom.subscribemenow.com/

CONTENTS

CHAPTER 1

On December the first, 1887, Susan Spencer reached out a trembling hand and collected her future from the agent across the desk. She could barely bring herself to look at the letter, but after taking a deep breath to steel herself, she unfolded it and read it swiftly, her brown eyes darting across the page. The words sifted in, each of them making up a meaning which, despite her hesitancy, came as no real surprise.

Zachariah Holden, aged forty-one, resident of Miles Gulch, Wyoming. A blacksmith. A few handwritten notes were scrawled at the bottom of the page; Zachariah Holden, unlike many men who applied to the matrimonial agencies, had taken the time to get references to his character from the townspeople who knew him best. The references were sparsely worded and badly spelled, but the mere fact that this

Mr. Holden had convinced busy farmers and store owners to write a word in his approval spoke volumes.

Susan looked back up at the agent, paused a moment, and then nodded.

"Very well," she said. "I accept."

The agent – a middle-aged woman with a matronly aspect that was belied by the fact that she was neither married nor an actual mother – smiled and nodded back.

"I'm very glad to hear it," she said. "We will send a telegram to Mr. Holden at once. He'll be delighted. He first wrote for a match some months ago, to our office in New York. They were unable to find a girl who was an appropriate match, and his letter was recently forwarded on here to Boston."

"Why were they unable to find a match?" Susan asked, her brow furrowing in slight suspicion.

"It happens at times," said the agent, waving a hand dismissively. "Perhaps no one was willing to leave so close to Christmas."

Susan bit her lip. The agent, avidly watching her reaction, leaned forward and said, "Of course, you've said that timing isn't an issue for you… Is that still correct?"

Susan nodded with a sigh.

"No, I don't mind leaving before Christmas."

In a way, it would be a relief – but she couldn't bring herself to inform the agent of this fact. It would be embarrassing to tell her of how depressing the last few years had been at Christmas time – every year, as the time wound close to the passing of her mother, her father sank a little deeper into his stupor. She did her best to care for him, trying to ignore the drinking and encourage him to take care of his health, but he had made it clear he no longer wanted to hear her "sanctimonious prattle."

Familial love had not done much for Susan Spencer; it had begun to make her bitter, and she desperately did not want to become bitter. She knew she had to leave before things got worse and she burrowed too deeply into her own aloof nature to ever return.

She had vivid memories of Christmases past, when her mother was still alive and relatively healthy, and her father had not yet succumbed to the slow, creeping sadness that started at the same time as his wife's heart problems. Susan could recall all too well the joy she had felt on getting out of bed Christmas morning, knowing her parents were waiting for her with love and affection and other things all wrapped up and tied with a bow. They were such a happy little family back then. It was shocking, and deeply saddening, to realize how much had changed in just the past handful of years.

In her heart, she knew she was just like any other woman: she wanted to find happiness and love, marry a good man who would treat her well, and raise a family. But the more she saw of her father's depression after the death of his wife, the more she feared it was in the blood somehow. Perhaps Henry had saved her from that same fate by leaving before they were wed…

She pushed the thought away hastily. It would never do to allow herself to become distracted with thoughts of Henry Hudson and the piece of Susan's heart he had taken with him when he left, seven years before. She had fought long and hard to move past him, and she couldn't let herself be derailed now.

Now that she was saying yes to starting again…

And right around Christmas, too. In fact – she brightened a little at the thought – perhaps, if the train was swift enough, she could even be married by Christmas Day.

"When should I prepare to leave?"

"Oh, as quickly as possible, dear. The later we get into the winter, the more difficulties may arise on your journey." The agent scrutinized her. "Would you be able to leave tomorrow?"

The suggestion took Susan aback. "Tomorrow?" she faltered, and sank back in her chair, clasping her hands in her lap. Chewing on her lower lip, she thought the proposition over. Yes, tomorrow was rather sudden; but, after all, there wasn't any reason why she couldn't go that quickly. After all – there wasn't anything holding her back or keeping her here in Boston.

Her father would raise a fuss, but it would pass quickly. He had no real attachment to her, she thought sadly.

And the memory of Henry Hudson – well, that was just a memory. Perhaps, when she left behind the streets they had once walked together, she would be able to forget about him once and for all.

"Yes," she said, decisively. "Yes, I can leave tomorrow. I'll buy a train ticket on my way home."

The agent beamed. Clearly, she was delighted this seemed to be working out so well both for Mr. Holden and Susan herself – the agency had a reputation for creating good matches, and Susan supposed that the apparent delay in finding a wife for Mr. Holden had caused something of a blot. Well, now she could fix that by agreeing to the swift arrangement – and facing her father with the news.

She gathered up the information the agent had prepared for her, said her thanks and goodbyes, bore the wishing of good luck, and left the office. The chilly Boston wind was blowing haphazardly down the street as she emerged, and she drew her coat around her, wishing she'd thought to wear her flannel scarf. Perhaps winter would not be so harsh in the territories – but she had no real hope of this. She'd heard plenty of stories about difficult living conditions in the west. It was a testament to her zeal for leaving Boston behind that she was willing to risk them since she had no particular liking for being uncomfortable.

A good life with a good husband would make up for all of that, she told herself as she hurried down the street. She could only pray it would turn out as she had hoped.

She stopped at the train depot and purchased her ticket, handing the money over with a little gulp of apprehension. It was more expensive than she had thought it might be – but again, she reminded herself, it would be worth it. The ends would justify the means.

Then, her gloved hands plunged deeply in her pockets to ward off the cold and clutching the ticket tightly, she hurried home.

Her father was asleep in the old armchair in front of the coal fire, his usual position these days. He startled awake as she entered and cast a dark look out the window at the encroaching dusk, which came on early these days.

"Where've you been, Susie? It's nearly dark."

"It's not so late as you think, Pa." Her father made an irritable gesture toward the twilight scene outside, and Susan hid a smile. "That's just the winter night for you. It's really not even gone five o'clock." She set her pocketbook down and came to stand near him, warming herself at the fire.

"You know, it's almost Christmas, Pa," she ventured, even now hoping that somehow this year would be different, that he would react with the warmth and cheer the holiday seemed to evoke in everyone else…

But she should have known better. He merely looked away from her, into the dancing flames. "Hmmph. Where were you all day, anyway?"

This was it, then. She would get no change from her father – and there was no point in holding on and hoping. She took a deep breath.

"I suppose I'd better come right out and tell you now," she said, "especially as I'm to leave tomorrow at noon. I've agreed to be matched with a man in Wyoming, Pa. He's a good man, a blacksmith. Hard-working, honorable. I leave tomorrow, and with any luck, the two of us will be married before Christmas."

She quieted down, realizing her father was staring at her with wide eyes.

"You ain't serious."

"I am, Pa."

"You can't go off and…" Her father gestured wildly. "Hogtie yourself to the first man you find, one you've never even met before."

"It isn't like that, Pa. I went to a matrimonial agency. I've been talking to them for over a week, now. They're very careful in who they accept as a client, and the matches they make."

"Pshaw!" Daniel Spencer made a violent gesture, throwing away her words. "I know what this is about – this is about that Hudson fellow who left you at the altar all those years ago."

Susan's heart felt as though it had suddenly iced over. A flush came to her cheeks, surely staining them a vivid red.

"It isn't about that at all," she said, striving to keep her voice calm. "And he didn't leave me at the altar. We discussed things and agreed to break it off long before it got that far."

"Nonsense. I was there, I remember it just as well as you do, and you're not going to convince me by pretending it was a small affair. That man ran off with some other woman and broke your heart. You've been stewing in your misery ever since, and now you've decided to take a pass on every other decent man in Boston and strike out west because you're afraid you'll end up a spinster."

Susan took a step back, shocked by the bitterness in her father's words. She took a few deep breaths, trying to wrap her mind around what he had said – and what it revealed about him. As sour and unhappy as she had known him to be, it was startling to hear him speak like this to his own, his only, daughter.

"If you want to talk about stewing in misery," she said, once she could control the levelness of her voice, "perhaps it's because you think everyone is content to be just as you are – unhappy and alone to the end of your days."

Her own voice was not kind, though it didn't quite meet the vitriol of her father's. In it she could hear reflected the bitterness she so desperately wished to avoid; in it, she could hear her own sadness and depression and the nightmares she still had from the time that her mother was dying. Susan had been away from home, working at the ladies' dress shop that was her first and only employment. Her father had gone out – she never found out what for – and had stayed out until dark. Until it was far too late…

Somewhere in the afternoon, Susan's mother had slipped into oblivion. Even now years later, Susan still had horrible dreams about her mother passing away, completely alone.

She tried to get ahold of herself, control her emotions, and carried on. "Well, you're wrong, Pa. I'm only twenty-six, and I'm not ready to give up on myself because I've been disappointed in love. I'm very sorry you feel this way – I had hoped that, at the very least, you would give me your blessing. But I'm too old to need your approval, and goodness knows I haven't depended on your help in any other way since Ma died."

She folded her arms and bit her lip, feeling tears strike hard at her eyes like needle pricks. "I'm going to Wyoming regardless of what you say. Only – Pa, I'm leaving tomorrow, and I did hope that you'd understand."

She turned away from him and faced the fire, embracing the warmth, wanting for nothing more than to have her coldness chased away. There was a long, quiet moment in which she could hear nothing but the crackling of the flames and the wood, and the breathing of the old man in the chair.

Then there was a creak as he stood up, and in the next moment he was standing by her, a hand on her arm.

"I do understand, daughter," he said; the cynicism was still in his voice, but it had been overshadowed by something else, something kinder. "I can't give you my approval because I don't approve. You're going to do it anyway – well, that's fine. That's the streak of stubbornness you inherited from me, not your mother. She was a fine woman – refined, too – and I never could understand why she would stoop down to take up with a nothing man like me."

He waited, but Susan couldn't bring herself to turn to him, and after a moment he gave a long, heartfelt sigh. "So you're leaving tomorrow," he said. "I suppose you know best what to do with yourself. It's your life, after all, and you shouldn't have to spend it in a drab little apartment in Boston caring for an angry old man with no joy left in life. You'll go west, Susan, and I hope you'll find more happiness than Boston has brought you. That's all the Christmas blessing I can give you, for I fear that the road ahead will be harder than you think."

She couldn't hold her tears in any longer; turning to him, she put her arms about his neck, and let him embrace her as he had done when she was a child – as he hadn't done since her mother had succumbed to her long illness and faded away into the dark.

Four years had passed since Susan's mother had fallen into her final sleep, and each year had been more and more difficult to traverse. Perhaps there was no saving Daniel Spencer from his life of sadness and misery –

But Susan was not beyond saving, not yet. And she was determined to save herself, if no one else was strong enough to take up the job.

CHAPTER 2

Susan's dreams of a happy Christmas carried her all the way across the country on the crowded, uncomfortable train. They soared her over the snow slide that blocked the tracks on the mountains; they kept her warm when the fireplace at one end of the car died because all the coal had been earmarked for the main engine itself. They sat beside her as she looked out the window at the swift-passing landscape, the wild beauty of the land sliding by, parts of the country she had never seen and had never truly believed she would see with her own eyes.

In the end, her dreams stepped down beside her as she disembarked from the train at her final destination: Miles Gulch, Wyoming, a bustling little town with its own big dreams. It was December the eighth. There were oil lamps and candles in every window, and happy families on every street, a large tree, well-decorated with tinsel in the town square, and snow falling gently in large flakes, gradually covering every flat surface in town. It was a perfect picture of the season, and she took a deep breath of the chill air, smiling to herself, before she struck out to find the blacksmith shop.

She had anticipated it would not be difficult to find, and she was correct in this. As a matter of fact, she located it only a few blocks away from the small depot. Already, she could hear the train whistling and puffing into motion, and her heart gave a leap at the knowledge that she had truly arrived. Any moment now, she would meet the man she was going to marry, this Zachariah Holden, and her life would change forever – for the better –

But something was off about the blacksmith shop, something that she could not quite put her finger on. Of course, there was the fact that the double doors were closed up tight. Well, perhaps he closed early some days; after all, it was already after four o'clock in the afternoon, and the dark was encroaching steadily. She looked over the tall house admiringly; it wasn't a new building, but it had been well-kept, and the knowledge that it was to be her new home thrilled her to the marrow. There were three stories; the shop itself must obviously take up the larger portion of the bottom floor, and she supposed the living quarters were on the next floor, with the tiny windows of an attic peeking out from above.

Taking her courage in both hands, she went to the smaller door at the edge of the house and knocked on it with a gloved fist.

Nothing but silence, utter silence from the house. She knocked again, and listened – in vain, though she strained her hearing for the slightest response. She stood for a moment more, unsure what to do, and then stepped back to look up at the windows. If they were open, perhaps she could shout and make herself heard…

But of course, they were not open, and she realized suddenly what it was that had struck her as so strange about the shop. The chimney at the top of the tall building was as dead and empty-looking as the house itself; there was no fire going on below.

But for a blacksmith's shop not to have any fire – she didn't know much about the industry, but she was rather certain that most men who worked at such jobs would keep their fires going at all times, even if banked down overnight. He wouldn't let it die out and start up again, coaxing it to rage every time he needed to shoe a horse or hone a knife – could he?

Susan chewed on her lip uncertainly. Surely, she was making too much out of this, she told herself. There must be something else at play here she didn't understand, that was all. And that was all right – she was used to not quite understanding things. But try though she might to tell herself that everything was going to turn out just fine, she couldn't shake the thought that something was terribly wrong.

She came to the door again and banged on it once more. Still no answer, not the faintest whisper of a sound. She glanced around – the neighboring buildings were quiet, as well. There were a few passers-by on the road, and she caught a curious glance from one of them as they went by. But she shrank back from asking for help until it was absolutely necessary.

Biting her lip, she turned back to the house and tried the door. To her surprise, the knob turned smoothly under her hand.

Before she knew it, she was standing in the opening of the blacksmith's shop. The shop itself spread out to her left, silent and dark and forbidding. In front of her was a narrow stairway. The only light in the whole place came from the windows set high in the walls.

"Hello?" she called, swallowing her fear.

There was nothing – nothing but an echo. Her own voice, bounding up the stairs and then back down to her, ghostly and strange…but with another element to it, too, something she couldn't quite comprehend.

"…lo…."

And then, so faint she could hardly believe she actually heard it, she caught the word,

"...please..."

Susan dropped her bags where she stood and ran up the stairs, not stopping to think about whether her hearing was playing tricks on her. At the top of the stairs she stopped, wide-eyed in alarm and fear. The blacksmith had generous living quarters up above his shop, with a kitchen directly in front of her and a neatly-appointed, if rather spare, sitting room adjacent to it.

Through the door she could see another door, one which she supposed to belong to the sleeping quarters. But her eyes were drawn to the man sprawled on his back across the sofa in the sitting room. He had a blanket drawn up to his chin and his teeth were chattering just above it from the cold. The fireplace was completely dead and by the looks of things, had been for some time.

"Oh, goodness."

Susan flew to his side, pressing her hand to his forehead. He had a high fever, which she would have guessed even had she not felt the heat for herself. The blacksmith was a ruin of a big man; his form under the blanket took up most of the sofa, but his face was sunken and sallow, and he had the look of someone who had been deathly ill for a very long time.

Hazy eyes focused blearily on her, and she said, in a low, hurried voice, "I'm Susan – Susan Spencer. The matrimonial agency sent me to you. You must be very ill…can you tell me what's wrong?"

The words that escaped him were difficult to understand, and he closed his eyes again immediately. His breathing was shallow; Susan's heart raced.

"I'll go and fetch the doctor," she said. "Stay here…"

The nonsensicalness of the words only struck her as she was running out of the room.

Now there was no point in avoiding the townsfolk that were passing by; she hadn't the faintest clue where the doctor might be, and time was of the essence. Racing down the street, feeling her hair coming loose from its pins, she flung herself at the first couple she saw.

"The doctor," she panted. "Where is the doctor?"

Bemused, the man stared at her, while his wife turned around and pointed behind them.

"Thattaway," she said. "About three blocks down."

"Thank you."

Susan flew past them, running as though her own life depended on it. She wasn't sure why she was so rushed in seeking out help for a man she scarcely knew; yes, they intended to marry each other, but that in itself couldn't explain the squeezing feeling at her heart, the feeling that told her there was much more at stake than just her nuptials. A man's life was hanging in the balance; he was likely to die, and he was lying there in his own home, completely alone…

Well, she wouldn't let it happen. Not if she could help it.

She found the doctor's office, flung open the door wide, and dragged the man out from behind his desk. It was fortunate for her – as well as for poor Zachariah Holden – that Doctor Stevens was both in the office and not currently engaged with a patient. She brought him back to the blacksmith shop, telling him what she knew in terse words, and then continuing on in swift silence. She was half afraid Zachariah would die before she returned.

She waited in the kitchen, biting her lip and with her back turned to the open door of the sitting room, while Doctor Stevens examined the blacksmith.

After what seemed an interminable time, he came back out and gave a deep long sigh.

"You'd best come in," he said. "I helped him into bed now, but I want to talk to you both."

Still chewing on her lower lip, she followed him, but hesitated just outside the bedroom door. It seemed impossible to set foot inside the inner sanctuary belonging to this man she did not even know; the doctor cast a puzzled, slightly irritated glance back at her, but stopped just inside the door and addressed them both.

"Mr. Holden is very ill. I suspect he has been for several days now, at least..." He cast a questioning glance at Susan, who shook her head to negate her own knowledge of the situation.

Dr. Stevens sighed. "I'd like to say that this isn't the worst case of the influenza that I've ever seen, but I'm afraid that it would be sugar-coating the truth to pretend such a thing. His fever is very high, and there is already some extensive damage to the body, perhaps even the brain." He turned more directly to Zachariah. "I've given you a dose of medicine, to help you sleep," he said, speaking clearly as though to a child. "Don't fight it – your body must rest."

Zachariah gave a wordless murmur.

"You'll look after him, I suppose?" Doctor Stevens inquired of Susan. She nodded, and he cast a glance over to her bags, which she had brought up with her.

"And while I'm asking questions, who, for that matter, might you be?"

"I'm..." She stopped suddenly. How to explain? She had no real right to be here – yes, she was engaged to him, but there was no legal arrangement yet. And suppose he didn't pull through the illness? What should she say?

But before she could gather her scattered thoughts, Zachariah Holden opened his eyes again and spoke. His voice was cracked and broken, but his words were unmistakable.

"Susan," he managed. And then, a few breaths later, "...wife...."

The doctor turned a stern glance on her. "His wife, eh?"

Susan opened her mouth to deny it – and then stopped short. If he pulled through, she certainly would be his wife before too long. If he did not – well, it was clear the poor man had no one else to care for him. If the doctor believed she was his wife, she could stay and take care of him throughout the course of the illness. He wouldn't have to die alone...

It wasn't such a terribly big fib, after all, though it did make her squirm.

"I – yes," she managed. "His wife."

"I see." The doctor sighed and rubbed at his eyes behind his thick spectacles. "Holden's only been here a year or two, and he always did play his cards close to his chest. I suppose it's not much of a surprise to find that he had a wife that we didn't know about until now. Well, I'm afraid that things are very bad, Mrs. Holden, very bad indeed." He took her arm and led her a little ways away from the sick bed. "I believe you should be prepared for the worst to happen."

Susan stared at him, wide eyed. "The worst…"

The doctor nodded, and she felt tears of sympathy prick her eyes. Of course, she hadn't met Zachariah Holden until that very afternoon – but still, what a terrible fate to occur to a man.

And if she told the doctor the truth, Zachariah would in all likelihood die all by himself, with no one at his side.

She steeled herself, and nodded understanding. "I see. Thank you for doing all you can, doctor."

He clasped her shoulder bracingly.

"Brave girl. So young, too – shall I send someone to sit with you? We have no nurses here in Miles Gulch, but my wife would manage to spare some time for you, I'm sure."

It was on the tip of her tongue to turn him down, telling him there was no need. Something made her stop, however. That was what the Susan who lived in Boston would have done, denying herself help and comfort when offered by others simply because she didn't feel she deserved it. But this wasn't Boston, and she had a feeling she wasn't really that same Susan anymore. She had met Zachariah Holden, the man she had agreed to marry – and everything had changed, even if not in the way she'd anticipated.

Instead of turning him down, she nodded.

"Yes, please," she said. "As you must realize, I'm rather new in town."

"Indeed. Well, I suppose you must have your own story – if you need a shoulder to cry on, my wife is very good at those sorts of things." He bent and took up his medical bag, casting Zachariah another glance and shaking his head. "Poor old Holden – we never did get to know him very well, and I suppose now we'll never get the chance." He turned his attention back to Susan. "Keep your chin up, girl. I don't think he's suffering much. I'll be back tomorrow with some more laudanum."

The word itself sent a cold dart into her heart; that was what her mother had been given, and in generous quantities, before she had died. Susan swallowed hard past the lump in her throat and nodded.

"I'll be here," she promised. "Right by his side."

"Good," said the doctor. "Take care of your health, mind. I don't need two deathly ill patients on my hands, especially not this close to Christmas."

Another solid squeeze of her shoulder, and then he was gone down the stairs, leaving Susan to stand and stare into the middle distance, trying to comprehend everything that had happened in the past few hours – and everything else that might happen very soon.

CHAPTER 3

On the tenth of December, Zachariah Holden died. He passed away in the middle of the afternoon, while he was sleeping peacefully. Susan was sitting by his bedside. Since the day she had arrived, she had scarcely gone anywhere else.

She was grateful for the townsfolk of Miles Gulch. Not only Mrs. Stevens, the doctor's wife, who had a more blessedly kindly bedside manner than her husband, but also her sister, Mrs. Falway. She and a cousin, Mrs. Tull, took turns in bringing meals and spending time with Susan. The result was that she now felt as though she at least had a few friends in the town she had hoped to call home; it was certainly an unexpected blessing, especially since everything else had been so frankly terrible.

As the doctor prepared Zachariah to be carried out, Susan sat at the kitchen table, staring mutely at the mug of tea in front of her. The whispers of the sweet ladies who had spent time with her over the past few days filled the edges of her hearing.

"Such devotion…I've never seen a wife who would so willingly spend every waking moment with her sick husband…and to think that Mr. Holden never even let on she existed."

The words made Susan's stomach twist within her. She felt riddled with guilt. Perhaps it wasn't such a big problem, in the scheme of things – and after all, it was due to Zachariah's words and the doctor's misunderstanding that anyone thought she was his wife at all. And even then, it was because of her desire to make sure he was cared for…plus, they would have been married if he had made it through the illness alive.

In fact, they might have already been married even now.

Still, she couldn't chase the feeling of guilt away entirely. She had allowed Doctor Stevens to carry on believing the untruth, to persist in his misunderstanding. And now, Susan was being lauded and praised for a wifely devotion she could not truly lay claim to.

Every urge within her told her she must go and set them straight, right this minute – but then what would she do?

The three women would surely tsk-tsk, disapproving of the fact she had stayed there alone to care for Zachariah. Susan felt no guilt about that – she was convinced she had done the right thing. Would they demand she leave town? Would they become cold and judgmental? She couldn't stand that, not right now when she was already feeling so terribly alone.

At a loss, she lifted the mug of tea to her lips and took a sip, just as Mrs. Stevens came in. The older woman wore a look of kindly concern, and she took a seat next to Susan and reached out to pat her hand.

"He's gone now, dear," she said gently. "They've carried him off to the undertakers – Mr. Palze understands the situation, and you needn't do anything just yet. Though he hadn't been here long, he was one of our own, and there's a pretty spot in the churchyard for him to rest, over by the oak trees. I'll take you there later so you can see for yourself. Father Taylor will say a service for him tomorrow."

Susan nodded and managed a grateful smile.

"Thank you – you've handled everything for me, and I appreciate it deeply."

"Not quite everything, Susan… you must decide what you would like to do, and I suggest that you make up your mind quickly so you're not traveling over Christmas." Another firm pat. "It wouldn't come as any surprise to the doctor and me if you decide to go back to Boston at once."

Susan stared at her with wide eyes. Up until now, she had put the thought of Boston out of her mind. To hear this possibility mentioned so casually took her aback; or, rather, the violence of her own emotional reaction to it took her aback.

"I don't want to go back to Boston," she burst out, and dropped her gaze to her hands as they lay on the table. "That is – certainly not right away. And perhaps not ever. There's nothing for me there."

"But surely you have family…"

"There's nothing for me there," Susan repeated firmly. She ventured to look back up at Mrs. Stevens. "Oh, can't I just stay here – at least for a little while?"

Mrs. Stevens made a doubtful face. "Why, of course you can stay here, dear – it's your home, after all."

Another consequence of masquerading as Zachariah Holden's legal wife suddenly became clear – she would inherit from him. The implications of this crashed in on her, one after another, and she held herself back from spitting out the truth – but only just. She held her tongue and listened as Mrs. Stevens continued, biding her time.

"Of course, the town will need another smithy before long – perhaps you can rent it out, if someone comes a-calling. Or you may decide to sell it with time. I understand this is a very difficult and delicate time for you, dear – no one would want to rush you into anything. Please, take your time. Don't make any hasty decisions."

One more firm pat and Mrs. Stevens stood. "There, now. I'll leave you to yourself for a little while, but if you get lonely, please come back to my husband's office and he'll send someone to fetch me. We've left you a meal for later; don't forget to eat. I'll come to collect you tomorrow morning and we can go to the service together. I'm sure you wouldn't want to be alone. I know I wouldn't at a time like this…"

She carried on, every word imbued with kindness, even as she left the kitchen and headed down the stairs. Susan followed her downstairs to the door and saw them all off, including the doctor who gave her an understanding nod. Then she closed the door behind them at last and turned around, feeling numb.

The silent shop gave her no comfort or answers; it gave her nothing at all.

What should she do?

What *could* she do?

One thing was certain: she was determined not to go back to Boston. Every day that passed by made her past life seem more like a prison from which she had escaped; it certainly hadn't been easy or worry-free to care for poor Zachariah, but at least she wasn't contending with a heavy-drinking or morose lay-about who felt he had the right to order her around.

Now here she was, in a house that, as far as the town was concerned, belonged to her. She could stay or she could go. She could rent, or sell, or do neither. She could do as she liked.

Though the idea was a welcome change, it didn't make her feel any more comfortable with the situation.

The only thing to do, she decided, was to wait it out, at least for the rest of the day. Perhaps the morning light would bring clarity to her thoughts as well as the rest of the world. Already, the twilight had fallen outside.

She ascended the stairs and lit candles and the oil lamp, desperate for a bit of cheer. She stirred up the fire in the little sitting room and sat by the window, looking out into the night, wondering what tomorrow would bring.

CHAPTER 4

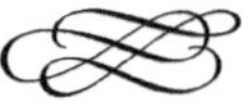

The morning brought the same troubles the previous day had brought, and the day after that followed suit. On December fourteenth, half driven crazy at last by her own indecision, Susan sought out the aid of Mrs. Stevens.

She found the good doctor's wife in their little cottage right in the heart of town. It was a frigid Thursday morning, and the doctor had gone on a house call several hours before. Mrs. Stevens invited Susan in gladly and sat her down with a cup of tea, and then commenced to listening.

Even as she spilled out her thoughts and worries and fears, Susan couldn't quite bring herself to let on that she and Zachariah had not really been married. She did slip in the fact that their connection had been facilitated through a matrimonial agency, however, and Mrs. Stevens nodded deeply as though this explained a great deal.

"I see, I see – I had thought that you seemed an odd couple, and I suppose that explains it." She chuckled at the look on Susan's face. "Now, I'm not saying anything bad about either you nor poor Mr. Holden – never speak ill of the dead, of course – but it's a fact that he's a good bit older than you, and I don't ever remember hearing that he had any connections in Boston. But if a matrimonial agency set the two of you up, well, now I can understand a little more. How long ago was that?"

"Er – not all that long, I suppose," Susan faltered, taken aback by the question. But her reaction didn't faze Mrs. Stevens in the least.

"I know how these things can be," she said kindly. "It's hard enough to remember my own birthday, let alone other such dates. And don't ask Doctor Stevens about such things, he'll only dismiss you out of hand for pressing him on things that don't matter a whit." She laughed. "Ah, well – men can be like that, I suppose. Well, the important thing, as you say, is to decide what your next step will be. Given that you're only recently arrived in town, I don't imagine that you feel much of a connection to Miles Gulch."

"On the contrary," said Susan, "I like it here very much. And – well, after all, you and your family have been very kind to me. And it's been a very long time since…since someone was that kind."

Mrs. Stevens' eyes softened with pity as they looked at her younger friend.

"Well, don't that beat all," she said gently. "I daresay you've got lots more kindness due to come your way, my dear. I'm sure we can find you a place to stay here in Miles Gulch, if that's what you want – or do you want to keep the smithy?"

Susan shook her head. "I don't know anything about blacksmithing, of course," she said. "I could rent it out, I suppose, but the apartment above is really designed to be lived in by the smith himself. Could I sell it?"

"You can certainly try," Mrs. Stevens said. "I'll ask Doctor Stevens to put the word out. I don't know of any smithy here in Miles Gulch that is looking for work, but perhaps in Millville or out toward Halftree way, there'll be someone who's willing to move in. In the meantime, you can stay there until something changes."

"But Zachariah didn't leave much money," Susan said, hoping that she didn't sound as though she were complaining – *never speak ill of the dead.* "And I have only a little myself, after the journey here. I've got to have some work, to have something to live on."

Mrs. Stevens nodded thoughtfully. Suddenly she snapped her fingers.

"I've got just the thing," she said, and stood up. "My dear, could I treat you to a tea at the local café?"

Susan looked down at the tea in front of her, and her older friend laughed.

"No, no – I mean a *real* tea."

Susan soon found out precisely what Mrs. Stevens meant. "A real tea" involved bundling up in coat and scarf and traipsing three blocks down and one block over to a high-class establishment run by a very genteel lady named Mrs. Caroline. Whether this was her first name or last name, Susan wasn't entirely sure, and the respectful but familiar way that Mrs. Stevens greeted her gave Susan no real clues. In turn, she greeted Mrs. Stevens with the same cordial familiarity, and told her to feel free to take her usual table.

"The finest tea establishment in Miles Gulch," Mrs. Stevens told Susan as they sat down in the corner. "Well," she amended, "granted, it's the only tea establishment in Miles Gulch. But all the ladies of the town come here at least once a week. It's the only respectable watering hole for a woman alone – of course, the Broken Thread Saloon is always open, but I certainly wouldn't advise you to go there without a gentleman to protect you. The fellows of Miles Gulch mean well, I'm sure, but a pretty little thing like you would be fair game as far as they were concerned, if you didn't have a husband to ward them off." She reached out and put a hand on Susan's, suddenly. "I'm sorry, dear, I didn't mean to upset you by referring to poor Zachariah…"

Susan hadn't even thought of it.

"Don't worry," she said, with a small smile. "I've been so diverted by your conversation that I've quite forgotten my own troubles."

"Such a brave girl," said Mrs. Stevens approvingly. "Of course, you won't want to even think about such things quite yet, but if you have a hankering to marry again, I'm sure Mr. Stevens and I would be happy to help you find a qualified candidate." She nodded and smiled at Mrs. Caroline, who set a silver tea service in front of them. "In the meantime, perhaps Mrs. Caroline here has already guessed why I've brought you along today."

Susan looked from one genteel lady to the other in confusion.

"Perhaps she has," she said. "But I thought it was just for tea…"

"What do you think?" Mrs. Stevens asked, directing the question to the owner of the tearoom. Mrs. Caroline folded her arms, tilted her head, and squinted at Susan thoughtfully.

"Have you any experience with serving tea?" she asked suddenly.

Susan gaped at her.

"Well, I – well, when we had guests to our family home, I did," she floundered. "I've never served tea in a commercial establishment like this…"

Mrs. Caroline waved a hand dismissively.

"Good," she said. "The worst thing is when girls come in thinking they know exactly what to do. I didn't become the owner of the finest tearoom in the west by hiring people who think they know better than their employer. I'd much rather train any girl who sets foot through my door, and that's a fact."

"Mrs. Caroline has been looking for help here," Mrs. Stevens explained to Susan. "When you mentioned needing a source of income, of course I thought of her."

The kindness of her new friend touched Susan's heart, and with difficulty she restrained herself from breaking down and crying a little. Instead, she clasped her hands together over her heart, and spoke with all her feeling.

"I'm delighted to be considered," she said simply. "And of course, I would do my best for you, Mrs. Caroline."

Mrs. Caroline nodded and then, to Susan's relief, gave her a kindly smile.

"I certainly could use the help with Christmas coming on," she said. "My regulars don't like having to wait too long to get their tea, especially in the cold weather. Come along tomorrow at about ten in the morning if you like. I'll give you a lesson before we open the doors."

She nodded once more to both women, and then marched off, straightening her already-straight apron, and went to her next table. Susan let out a breath.

"Goodness. I didn't realize I was going to have a job interview."

Mrs. Stevens laughed.

"That's the best way," she said. "It keeps you from getting overly nervous. You'll do fine, my dear. And with a little income and the smithy to stay in until it sells, I've no doubt that you'll have a wonderful Christmas here in Miles Gulch."

CHAPTER 5

Susan settled into working at Mrs. Caroline's finest tea establishment with more alacrity than she would have expected. The lessons in how to serve the tea were simple enough; Mrs. Caroline didn't want any fancy flourishes.

"Just a plain, straightforward pour," she directed. "Neatly well-done. We are a town of simple but civilized folks, Mrs. Holden. Tea is one of the gifts of the benevolent Creator, but that doesn't mean it needs all the foofaraws people out east might include."

Susan wasn't entirely sure what foofaraws Mrs. Caroline was referring to – what did she think people back east put in their tea? It was a mystery – but she pretended to know exactly what was being discussed and nodded wisely. It seemed best, under the circumstances, especially since Mrs.

Caroline knew full well that Susan herself was from "out east." For the first time, Susan wondered if the people of Miles Gulch viewed her with suspicion, simply for being an outsider – and if the stout support of people like Mrs. Stevens was the only thing that was keeping her in the good graces of the town.

That gave her even more reason to be grateful for her friends.

On the second day, the beautiful – if cold – weather gave way to snow clouds that dropped an inch or two over the course of an hour. Only a few ventured out for tea that day, and Mrs. Caroline frowned thoughtfully as she looked out the window and up and down the street.

"I do hope that the weather hasn't impacted too many of my regulars badly," she said. "If they've decided to stay at home, I can't blame them – but if they started here and slipped and fell, I doubt that Doctor Stevens could tend to them all."

Her concern was simultaneously touching and amusing; it was clear she believed only the worst of environmental circumstances could possibly prevent her loyal customers from coming to their tea. Susan hid a smile, and Mrs. Caroline sighed.

"Ah, well," she said. "As we are so quiet today, Mrs. Holden, perhaps you would be so good as to assist me with decorating? I've been so busy that I haven't had time for it yet."

Susan didn't need to be asked twice. The interior of the tearoom was pleasant and quaint, but it seemed to cry out for the greenery and lights of the holiday. She spent the rest of the afternoon pinning up wreaths and garlands, setting up candles and oil lamps, and decorating the small tree that waited patiently in the corner furthest from the fireplace. As she worked, she hummed a popular tune to herself; after a while, the thought struck her that Mrs. Caroline might not appreciate popular music, and she darted a glance to her employer to gauge her reaction. But Mrs. Caroline caught her look and gave her an encouraging nod and smile. So encouraging, in fact, that Susan took heart and began to sing the words to another song she'd heard shortly before her journey west.

She had finished that one – to a round of polite applause, to her surprise – and was embarking on "I Gave My Love A Rose" when the door opened, and Mrs. Caroline stood up with a cry of decorous delight.

"Why, Mr. Hudson. And Lucy, too. What an unexpected surprise."

"Why, of course, Mrs. Caroline. On a day like this, what else is there to do but go to tea?"

Susan's heart skipped a beat at the mention of his name, but it wasn't until she heard the deep tones of a voice that was all too familiar that she froze in the middle of her hanging another ornament. Eyes wide, she could do nothing but stare at the green fronds just in front of her, though they turned blurry from the closeness of her examination.

It couldn't be.

But she was sure of it. She was sure that it was him…

But how? Her mind raced even as she argued with herself, trying to tell herself that the truth she knew could not be so. It was as plain as the nose on her face, or the needles before her eyes, that Henry Hudson had just set foot inside Mrs. Caroline's tearoom. And yet she could not bring herself to believe it. She wouldn't believe it until she saw him. And she refused, absolutely refused, to turn around. If she never laid eyes on him, then it couldn't be him…

"I do believe you've acquired a helper, Mrs. Caroline, since we were here last."

"A new employee," said Mrs. Caroline, the warmth in her voice betraying how she had already grown quite attached to Susan. "Mr. Hudson, Lucy, allow me to introduce Susan Holden. Turn around, please, Susan, and greet our guests."

Gritting her teeth, trying to control her stuttering heart, Susan did as she was asked. It still took a moment yet before she could bring herself to raise her eyes to the man who stood before her, and when she did, she was somewhat gratified to see the stark astonishment on his face. It was some consolation that Henry Hudson was as startled as she was to suddenly be in company with her again.

Startled – but perhaps not as dismayed. Though there was no denying the shock in his dark eyes, there was also no denying the fact that a grin broke out across his face almost immediately. And the shock was accompanied by a fire-lit glow of warmth that brought a blush to her face.

Why, he looked – glad to see her.

And, she had to admit, handsomer than ever. The intervening seven years between the end of their courtship and this unexpected reunion had been kind to him. He must be, oh, thirty-one or thirty-two by now – but the lines on his face, carved by unknown events and sadnesses, had only added to his appeal. He had always seemed a self-assured man, attractive in his own confidence; she hated to feel the stirring of the same old feeling of being drawn toward him, even after all this time.

"As a matter of fact, Mrs. Caroline, we need no introduction. Susan – that is, Mrs. Holden and I are old friends."

The audacity of this made Susan lift her chin and square her shoulders.

"Friends, Mr. Hudson?"

His dark eyes were laughing at her now. "Perhaps that's not the word you would have chosen."

"Indeed not."

"Well," said Mrs. Caroline, who was trying to conceal her quivering curiosity under an extra-thick layer of gentility, "do you know Mr. Hudson or not, Mrs. Holden?"

"We were acquaintances in the past," said Susan, with as much dignity as she could muster. "I did not know he was here in Miles Gulch."

Henry Hudson didn't appear to be forthcoming with the details of his current existence, seeming content just to smile at Susan, so Mrs. Caroline filled the gap.

"He is rather new in town – only the past few years, isn't that right, Mr. Hudson? He moved here with his daughter, Lucy." Mrs. Caroline gave the little girl next to Mr. Hudson a warm smile. Susan realized, with another sense of surprise, that she had scarcely even noticed the girl, she'd been so taken aback by Henry Hudson's presence. Now she saw that the girl – Lucy – was six or seven, though she appeared small for her age. Her hair was a dark brown and her eyes, too, were the same wide, dark eyes as her father, fringed with thick black lashes. She was an adorable little girl, a clear descendant of Henry Hudson but with a delicacy that must come from her mother.

Her mother – the woman that Henry had left Susan for, all those years ago. Was the woman herself about to walk in and join her family for tea? Susan didn't think her heart could handle it.

The reminder was painful, but Susan scolded herself for ignoring the little girl. After all, it wasn't her fault. And it wasn't her fault that she reminded Susan so much of her father, either. To make amends, Susan came forward and got to her knees to be at the child's level, giving her the warmest smile she could manage and holding out her hand.

"Good morning, Lucy. My name is Susan – I'm new here in town."

Lucy responded to this display of friendliness with a shy smile. She twisted her hands together for a moment in doubt before she received a nudge from her father, prompting her to take Susan's hand and shake it swiftly before dropping it and backing up a step or two. Still, the smile remained, and it was clear that she was rather intrigued by Susan.

Before she could stop herself, Susan glanced up – and her eyes caught those of Lucy's father. Immediately, he held a hand out to help her up from the floor. For a split second she revolted against the very idea of accepting any help from Henry Hudson; but her winter skirts were heavy, and it would have been far worse to stumble as she stood up. Clenching her teeth, she took his hand and stood up, then dropped it even faster than Lucy had dropped hers.

"Well," said Mrs. Caroline, taking over the flow of the conversation – much to Susan's relief. "Please feel free to sit at your usual table, Mr. Hudson – as you can see, the inclement weather has prevented many others from venturing out today. We will be free to tend to your needs, and tea is practically in your cups as we speak."

Henry Hudson gave an appreciative nod and a smile to his hostess, but his eyes had once again strayed to Susan. She turned away abruptly and went into the little kitchen to tend to the tea.

Mrs. Caroline followed her.

"Mrs. Holden, far be it from me to poke my nose in where it isn't wanted – but I have to ask, as you are my employee and Mr. Hudson is a guest here. Is everything – quite all right?"

Susan heaved a long sigh, feeling rather grateful that Mrs. Caroline had picked up on the uncomfortable emotions between them. Still, she couldn't drag the poor woman into her own drama; besides, Mrs. Caroline was far too genteel and fine to understand being practically left at the altar.

Susan could hardly understand it herself. For months, Henry had courted her, and she had been thoroughly in love by the time he asked her to marry him. But he hadn't yet asked her father, and she had requested that he do so first. Her father would be more than willing to hand her off, she was sure of it; her mother, who had not yet passed away at the time, simply adored Henry, and could not approve of the match more.

She had never found out exactly what happened. Henry had spoken with her father, and suddenly everything had changed. The very next day, he told her that he had made a mistake, and that he was traveling west to meet and marry his second cousin, a match of which his own parents had approved. He was gone within the week, leaving Susan heartbroken and bereft, and she had never heard of him again…until now.

The thought that he had been cheerfully living his life with his new wife and daughter, out here in the west, while she had been languishing away in Boston slowly losing her joy – well, it was even more painful to realize.

Worse than that, though, was this certainty in the pit of her stomach that her affection for Henry had somehow not been destroyed by his actions. Even now, knowing that he was sitting in the next room, she had butterflies in her stomach. Did that make her a bad person? A fallen woman – someone who still harbored feelings of love for a married man? She shrank away from the thought.

And she certainly couldn't explain any of that to Mrs. Caroline. So she said, "There's nothing to worry about," and her employer simply nodded and accepted her words.

With the fine, genteel touch that was typical of her, however, she took the tea out and waited on Henry Hudson and his daughter herself, without asking that Susan do so.

Susan watched from behind the door, observing how Henry interacted with his daughter. There was no denying the fondness on his face; it gave her heart a twinge to see it. He was clearly meant to be a father. She couldn't regret that or be jealous of it. Lucy, despite her shyness, was one of the happiest children Susan had ever seen.

Again, she wondered where Lucy's mother was. When Mrs. Caroline returned, she ventured to ask about it, keeping her voice low.

"Ahh," said her employer, shaking her head sadly. "That poor man – and poor Lucy. I understand that Mrs. Hudson passed away shortly before they moved here. A sudden illness – I don't believe she was a very strong woman, and I'm afraid that her fragility has been passed on to her little girl. He doesn't speak of her often – it can't have been more than three years."

Three years – which meant that Lucy had been only three, perhaps, when her mother died. Despite her complicated feelings, Susan's heart went out to the little girl – and to her father, who had lost someone he loved. Susan knew all too well what it was to lose a mother. And, to her regret, she knew what it was to lose the one she loved with all her heart, too. After all, Henry Hudson himself had been lost – no, not lost. He had turned his back on her. Perhaps it wasn't the same thing, but the feelings were still similar, and Susan was not a vindictive person. She regretted that Henry had caused her so much pain, but she wouldn't wish that same pain on him or anyone.

As she watched them, she saw Henry's eyes dart toward the entryway to the little kitchen. He was looking for her, perhaps wondering whether she would return to serve them. Well, she would keep well back so he didn't see her, and she wasn't about to go out there unless Mrs. Caroline asked her to do so.

She was certain he couldn't see she was there, but that didn't explain why suddenly, when looking in her direction, a warm smile spread across his handsome face as though he couldn't help himself.

Well. Now she knew that she shared her new town with her old flame. And though her life had been marked by tragedy ever since they had parted, it was evident he had not escaped unscathed, either. She could not put her finger on precisely how she felt about the matter, or about his presence – and she could not for the life of her determine whether it was better or worse that Henry Hudson was here, a widower – and free to remarry.

It didn't matter one way or another, she told herself sternly. She had certainly moved past that portion of her life, and she was a different person now than she had been seven years ago. She was determined to make her life anew here in Miles Gulch, regardless of whether Henry Hudson was here or not.

His presence made no difference to her plans.

At least, that was what she told herself, more than once all through that snowy morning.

CHAPTER 6

A few days later, Mrs. Caroline took ill.

"It's nothing," she told Susan, waving a hand. "Simply a head cold."

But it was clear she was miserable.

"Perhaps it is nothing," Susan told her, "but you really ought to be in bed. It's going to snow again today, look – and that means it'll only get colder. You shouldn't risk your health by venturing out or being around others. I can fetch what we need at the store, and then I can help your guests on my own."

"Oh, pshaw."

"Please, Mrs. Caroline, please go and lie down. You're only in the back rooms – if I need help, I can call you."

Her employer considered the matter for a moment. It was evident that she felt much worse than she claimed, for she allowed Susan's arguments to sway her, and she acquiesced.

"But please don't neglect to call me before things get out of hand," she said as she went through the door to her quarters, as though the tearoom was just as likely to break out in a brawl as the saloon down the street. Susan reached for her coat, glancing at the grandfather clock in the corner. If she hurried, she could get the sugar that was so sorely needed and make it back before the first guests arrived.

Although, she reckoned as she walked swiftly down the street, it looked to be another day in which hardly anyone would venture out. If she hadn't had to go to the mercantile, she certainly would have stayed indoors. It wasn't actually snowing yet, but the threat was undeniably there, and the clouds hung heavily overhead. As it was so dark, even at ten in the morning, there were candles burning in every window along the street, giving a cheerful and festive air to the little town. Susan pulled her coat about herself a little more tightly and hurried a bit more, thinking of all the things she had to do that day with Mrs. Caroline indisposed.

She had made her purchase and half-run back to the tearoom, but there was still someone waiting at the front door. A small someone – a child – Lucy Hudson.

"Goodness, Lucy. You must be freezing, poor thing. Come along inside and stand by the fire for a moment to warm up."

Susan bustled the little girl, unprotesting, into the tearoom and established her on the chair nearest the fire.

"I'm sorry I wasn't in when you arrived – I had to fetch some sugar for your tea. I didn't know you'd be coming today." She glanced warily around the room as though Henry Hudson had somehow slipped in without her noticing. "Your father isn't with you?"

Lucy shook her head. Her shyness had not yet dissipated, but she was still obviously intrigued by Susan, and gave her a starry-eyed gaze that was as eloquent as a full paragraph. Susan stopped bustling and smiled back at her, then sat down across from her and reached out to put a hand over the little girl's.

"Are you allowed to venture out on your own, Lucy?"

Lucy nodded.

"I can come to Mrs. Caroline's when Pa's at work," she said. "He said I could."

"All right, then. Just so long as you have your Pa's permission – I don't want to worry him."

"He'll come fetch me when he's ready for dinner," the little girl said candidly. "He works very hard."

"I'm sure he does."

"He's the strongest worker at the mill. Mr. Oliphant says so."

"And who is Mr. Oliphant?"

"Pa's bosser."

Susan chuckled.

"You mean his employer?"

Lucy's brow wrinkled in thought. "I don't know," she said, "he bosses Pa all right."

Susan laughed outright.

"I'm glad to hear it. I reckon your Pa could do with some bossing." She caught herself then, with a swift internal reminder that she no longer knew Henry Hudson – she herself had said they were nothing more than old acquaintances. Still, the temptation to speak about him to his daughter was stronger than she could resist. "Does he enjoy his work?"

Lucy gave a little shrug.

"He'd rather be home with me, he says."

"I'm sure of it."

"But when we're home, he looks sad anyhow, and then he takes me to Mrs. Caroline's, or out to the pond to go skating, or to the mercantile, or to visit the Childers down the street. Anne is my best friend," Lucy confided. "She's two years older than me, and she can sew a whole dress for her dolls."

Susan smiled, though her heart was twisting within her. The unassuming, candid little insight into the life of Henry Hudson and his daughter was touching, but she felt suddenly as though she had looked through a keyhole into a room where she didn't belong. What right had she to interrogate his daughter about him? What right had she to anything?

Her moral dilemma was interrupted by the front door, as a few more brave souls ventured out into the weather in search of tea. The rest of the morning was blessedly busy, as she cared for the needs of all without resorting to bothering Mrs. Caroline, who was evidently getting some much-needed rest. Through it all, she caught glimpses of Lucy Hudson, who had brought some paper and a pencil with her and was busily drawing, humming to herself and kicking her legs in the air. Evidently, she was quite accustomed to spending time alone here at Mrs. Caroline's.

A few hours later, when the rush was over, Susan was startled to realize it was nearly one o'clock. Just as she was about to ask Lucy when her father might be coming for her, the door opened and the man in question entered.

The tearoom was empty except for the three of them, and Henry Hudson paused just inside the door, his hand still on the knob, and gazed at Susan. She couldn't help but be arrested by his gaze; they stood stock still for a long moment, frozen in a tableau, their gazes communicating far more than their words ever would - and then Henry shook himself and entered the room fully, closing the door behind him to block out the frigid drafts.

"There she is." he said, rubbing his hands together and advancing on Lucy. "I had a feeling I'd find you here, even though it is snowing outside."

"I was a bit worried to find her here on her own." Susan heard the reproach in her voice, and winced at it, but she couldn't seem to get rid of it now. No, she simply had to carry on as though she had the right to lecture Henry Hudson about his parenting. "She assured me that she had permission to venture out on her own, but I was very concerned about her doing so on a day like this."

"She likes to spend time with Mrs. Caroline," Henry said, glancing up at her and then just as swiftly looking back down at his daughter. "Especially around Christmas, isn't that right, Lucy?" Another glance at Susan. "I encourage her to come here if she gets cold. Sometimes I leave early, before she's awake, and the fire goes out."

"You should get a nanny for her," Susan blurted out, regretting it instantly. There was a long pause, and then Henry turned back to her.

"I've been thinking about that," he said. "Of course, it's difficult to do in a town like this – but a few kindly souls have recommended asking a neighbor to keep an eye on her. There's always Mrs. Childers, but she's got a brood of her own. And then there's another option that a few have mentioned…" His dark eyes met hers. "Perhaps I'll marry."

Susan felt a squeezing sensation in the pit of her stomach, something akin to panic. There was a heavy import in his gaze, but she didn't understand it. All she knew, with a suddenness that startled her, was if Henry Hudson married someone else, and she was there to see it, she could not possibly stay here in Miles Gulch. It was bad enough that he was here to begin with. It was bad enough that his daughter was so precious and sweet. It was bad enough that he'd had a good life with the woman he'd left Susan for. But to stand by and watch him choose someone else again was too much to ask of anyone.

"I suppose that's your business," she said stiffly. "Myself, I would think one marriage would be enough for anyone."

"Well," said Henry with a small smile, "one at a time, certainly."

Lucy piped up, "Pa, can Susan come for Christmas dinner?"

Her father glanced back down at her with a warm smile.

"Lucy, you know we're going to the Childers for Christmas dinner."

"Yes – can Susan come?"

Henry chuckled. "I don't think it's polite to invite people to the homes of others, but I'll certainly ask Chuck and Mrs.

Childers." His eyes returned to Susan. "That is – if Susan thinks she would like to come with us."

Susan didn't know what she thought. It was suddenly sinking in that perhaps, just perhaps, Henry's meaningful look as he spoke about marriage actually meant that he was referring to *her* as his potential bride. She didn't want to think it – she didn't dare allow herself to believe it for a moment. But now he was asking her to spend Christmas with them. Her complicated feelings were certainly not getting any less tangled the longer she was in his presence.

"I'm afraid I can't say one way or another," she said. "I may be busy then." It was one of the weakest protestations she'd ever given, and she hastened to add, "My home is up for sale, you see, and I'm hoping it will sell before Christmas. I may be involved in moving house at the time."

"I see. I wondered what your circumstances were – I admit that I was almost unforgivably nosy and thought about asking around to see what the gossip might be." Henry grinned at her. "But I restrained myself."

Well, he had done better than she had, Susan thought, biting her lip.

"May I ask how you came to be here in Miles Gulch?"

Susan lifted her head, trying to regain her composure. It was almost impossible under the weight of his gaze.

"As a matter of fact, I answered a letter for a Mail Order Bride last month," she said. "For poor Zachariah Holden."

"Ah, the smithy. Sad state of affairs. I'm sorry for your loss. And that's why your home is for sale." He nodded, rubbing his chin. "I suppose you'll move on from Miles Gulch, then. Where will you go?"

"I had rather hoped to be able to stay. I like Miles Gulch, and I've made some kind friends here." She glanced quickly at Lucy and gave the little girl a smile. Lucy smiled back, her eyes lighting up.

"Then you can come for Christmas." she said.

"Perhaps I may," Susan told her, unwilling to crush the little girl's generous spirit. "But I cannot promise anything. I'd hate to go back on a promise."

Her eyes darted swiftly to Henry, just in time to see a cloud overshadow his face. The jab was clearly felt.

But he did not comment on it, choosing instead to say, "I'm sure Zachariah would have wanted you to stay, too, if that's what you want. Something will work out – though I'm sorry for your loss, and so soon after your arrival. Still, perhaps it's better that way – less painful."

Something about his words struck her, and she realized suddenly that her own confession may have been too much. The rest of the town believed she and Zachariah had been truly married, even if living separately for a time – but she could tell Henry believed no such thing.

"It's still…rather painful," she said, wondering wildly whether she could cover it up without an outright fib.

"You must not have known him for very long. And surely it's worse to lose a husband than to lose a man you were only briefly engaged to."

"I…I…I never said we were only briefly engaged…"

"No," said Henry, "but you did say that you only answered his letter last month. That sounds rather brief to me – Mrs. Holden. Or should I say Miss Spencer?"

"I don't think you should feel so free to assume anything about my marital status, that's all."

"Are you suggesting that your marriage was conducted by some sort of correspondence course?" He tilted his head curiously, but his eyes were sparkling with humor.

"No, I just…" She didn't know what to say. "I may not have known Zachariah for very long, or very well – but I cared for him in my own way. And I was there for him when he slipped away from this life. You, of all people, should understand how that feels."

Henry sobered instantly, but instead of the anger that she feared might show up, his eyes were filled with compassion and contrition.

"You're right," he said. "I do understand how that feels – and I'm very sorry, again, for the pain Zachariah's death has caused you. Regardless of your marital status, it must be a heavy disappointment to have lost someone you intended to spend your life with."

She didn't want to look at him, but she couldn't help herself. Once again, her eyes were drawn to his and fixed there, reading in the depths of his soul all the pain and understanding that they shared.

"Perhaps," he said softly, "you will find it in your heart to start again."

CHAPTER 7

Five days before Christmas, Susan glanced up as the door to the tearoom swung open, and saw a stranger enter. He was a tall, handsome stranger, if a bit grizzled; his arms were huge, his frame stalwart, and she caught herself staring openly at the broadness of his shoulders.

The stranger glanced around the room, and then seemed to fixate on her. He moved in her direction with a slow, sure step, and gave her a smile that made her take a step back. He looked so intent that it was almost disturbing – and rather flattering at the same time.

"Susan Holden?" he said.

"Er – yes," Susan said. Even after the several days she had been here, she was still thrown off somewhat by being referred to by a married name – especially one to which she had no true claim.

The stranger extended his hand for her to shake. She took it, half expecting her hand to be crushed in his grip. But she was surprised; his hand was large and rough, it was true, but warm and gentle for all that, and he held her hand in his as though he were accompanying her to a dance.

"I'm Ross Wilson. Doc Stevens told me to look for you here. I'm the blacksmith out at Halftree, and I understand you're looking to sell your husband's spot."

"Oh, a blacksmith." she said. "That explains it, then…"

Ross Wilson tilted his head at her curiously.

"Explains what, Mrs. Holden?"

"Oh, dear." She fought a blush; she couldn't, she just couldn't, tell this man she didn't know that she was referring to the broadness of his shoulders and the muscles of his arms. Goodness, but she didn't know what got into her sometimes. "It explains…why you're looking for me, I mean. How kind of Doctor Stevens to reach out to you. Yes, the town needs a new blacksmith." She laughed, though she feared it sounded rather forced and strangled due to her confusion. "And I certainly won't fit the bill."

Ross Wilson smiled at her. His eyes were light blue and very kind.

"I dunno about that," he said. "I've only just met you, but I reckon you could do just about anything you set your mind to, Mrs. Holden."

Another blush met the first as it was descending.

"If you care to sit and take some tea," she said, "I'll be finished here shortly, and I can take you over to show you the place."

"I'm not much for tea – but I spotted the saloon down the street on my way here. I'll stop in there for a bit if you don't mind." He read the expression on her face, and added, "Don't worry about coming in to fetch me, if you object to it. I'll watch for you. I reckon a pretty little thing like you doesn't venture into places like that too often."

How was it possible to blush three times at once?

She acquiesced with a murmur that made little, if any, sense, and returned to her work. Her mind was racing; half of it was preoccupied with the prospect of selling her home and finding somewhere new to live in Miles Gulch. The other half was pondering gleefully over how handsome the new blacksmith was and how obvious his attention to her had been. She found herself regretting, absurdly, that Henry Hudson had not been present at the time.

After the dinnertime table setting, she met Ross Wilson outside the saloon. He greeted her with a smile and held out an arm for her to take. She didn't need a second thought.

Together, they strolled down the street in the direction of the smithy, and she was immensely gratified, just before they turned the corner, to see that none other than Henry Hudson had just come out of the mercantile, and he was staring in their direction.

Sometimes, she wondered very much whether she was truly a good person, to have such a jubilant spirit over the idea of making someone jealous.

But she couldn't help it. She favored Ross Wilson with a smile, and he warmed up to it as though she had given him an outrageous compliment.

"I hear you're new in town," he said. "And recently widowed, forgive me mentioning it."

"Oh," she said. "And who did you hear this from?"

"I asked around about you at the saloon," he confessed candidly. "Couldn't help myself – I had a mighty powerful curiosity about why such a pretty woman was alone and selling a blacksmith shop."

"And was your curiosity satisfied?"

"Nearly," he said. "I guess there was one or two questions that I didn't get answered yet."

"Oh? And what were those, Mr. Wilson? Perhaps I could help you with them."

"Call me Ross," he said. "And I've no doubt you could – but they can wait a while. Is this it?"

She led them to the house and unlocked the front door to let him in. He made his way unerringly to the shop itself and flung wide the large double doors. With a practiced eye, he looked around the shop space, his arms folded and face set in a study. Susan watched him; his shoulders really were enormous, and he took up the space in the shop as though it were made for him.

"I'm sorry it's so cold," she said. "I haven't started the fire down here since – well, since poor Mr. Holden passed away."

"I don't blame you. I reckon there are some painful memories here."

"It's very sad to think of how Zachariah was so sick," she acknowledged, but felt compelled to add, "my heart went out of him, of course, though we truly did not know each other very well."

Ross Wilson glanced over at her. The expression on his face hovered between puzzlement and an attempt at understanding.

"I guess arranged marriages can be like that, sometimes," he said.

Susan bit her lip. It had been on the tip of her tongue to confess the truth to him – but if he'd already been told she and Zachariah had really been married, she couldn't very well set him straight without the rest of the town finding out. The thought of it made her squirm. She truly hated that the good people of Miles Gulch believed a falsehood about her, even if she hadn't been the one to spread the lie in the first place. But she had gone too far to back out now – at least, not yet. Someday, surely, she would have to face the consequences of allowing everyone to call her Mrs. Holden when she had no legal claim to it.

But…not yet.

"Well," said Ross, completing his inspection of the shop and returning to her, "I reckon it's worth at least what you're asking for – if not more. Your husband kept his tools in good order, too. I've lived in Halftree for my whole life, Mrs. Holden, and at thirty-five I'm just about ready for a change." He smiled at her. "Maybe more than one change."

His attention was no less flattering now than it had been earlier in the day.

"You'd like to buy the shop?"

"I would." He glanced upwards at the ceiling. "I reckon I'll wait to look at the quarters upstairs until another day. I'd never want to impose on a woman."

"Perhaps I'll invite you to tea soon," she said spontaneously, and then backtracked as she remembered his beverage preferences. "That is…"

"Tea would be much appreciated," he said, grinning, "provided it's with you. It's not about what you're drinking, it's about who you're drinking it with."

"Thank you," she said, dropping her gaze to the ground, unable to face up to his meaningful glance any longer. She had never had a man flirt with her quite so forwardly; even Henry Hudson had taken his time. "How soon would you move in?"

"Well, my lease is up on the Halftree shop, and I have the money to buy this place outright."

"Oh…"

He studied her for a moment.

"That being said," he continued, "I'd never demand that a woman move out of house and home in the middle of the winter – and especially not before Christmas. I don't suppose you've got a place to go yet."

"Not quite, no. I've been asking around, and I'm certain that I'll find something soon."

"Right, then." He nodded and granted her another warm smile. "Let's say that you can just stay put until that happens, and in the meantime, I'll put myself up at the inn and get to work. That is, if you don't mind a little hammering from down below – and a big, dirty fellow wandering in and out at all hours."

Susan laughed at his description of himself and wondered why yet another blush was steadily making itself felt.

"The town will be glad to have you," she said. "And so will I."

"Then that's all that matters. And maybe that answers my other questions, too." He fished an oilskin wrap from his pocket and handed it over to her. "Your payment."

Suddenly, with the bills in her hand, she felt at a loss – almost guilty. She couldn't help but stare at them. This money represented the blacksmith shop, it was true; it represented her future. But it also represented the lie that she had allowed to be told about her relationship with Zachariah Holden. It represented how much she was claiming without being entitled to a bit of it.

It threw her into a confusion that she knew she couldn't recover from while she was in Ross Wilson's presence.

Not daring to meet his gaze, she spoke without raising her head.

"I'd better see to my meal and then get back to work, Mr. Wilson. Can you find your way back to the inn?"

She could hear the puzzlement in his voice when he spoke.

"I surely can, Mrs. Holden. I – I hope everything's all right."

"Yes – yes, everything is fine. It's just…a bit overwhelming."

"Why, sure," he said gently, and put a hand on her shoulder. "You just keep on doing what you're doing, Mrs. Holden. Everything will turn out fine."

She finally managed to look up as he left the blacksmith shop. Though he did not turn to see it, her eyes were full of gratitude.

CHAPTER 8

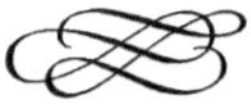

Three days before Christmas, Susan was leaving the tearoom in the late afternoon, ready to head home and turning anxious eyes to the gray skies above, when Henry Hudson appeared out of nowhere and hailed her.

"Susan."

Susan turned to the door, making a show of ensuring that it was closed as she muttered, "Oh, dear…" to herself. When she had composed herself – at least, as composed as she ever got when Henry was around – she turned back and gave him a very small smile. The smallest she could manage, as a matter of fact.

"Good afternoon, Mr. Hudson. Where is Lucy?"

"She's at Mrs. Childers, decorating gingerbread cookies with Anne and the other kids. The closer we get to Christmas, the more excited she becomes." He folded his arms and looked down at her. The expression on his face was difficult to read but seemed to suggest that he was searching for something – she didn't know what. "I've hardly seen you the past few days."

"I've been very busy."

"Lucy and I came in for tea yesterday, but you weren't here."

"Mr. Hudson, I rather resent the implication that I have to explain my whereabouts to you. You are not my father."

He took a step back.

"You're right – I'm sorry, Susan. I guess I was just worried. And Lucy wondered where you might be…and whether you're still coming to Christmas dinner with us." He eyed her. "Or have you forgotten?"

"Of course, I haven't forgotten," she grumbled, turning away and beginning to head in the direction of home. Henry fell into step beside her. "But I'm not entirely certain whether I'll be free to come. I told you both, I'm rather busy with the sale of the shop."

"Yes, I know. I heard about Mr. Wilson's arrival. It's good that it'll work out, I reckon. But I hope it won't keep you from Christmas dinner." He paused a moment. "And I hope nothing else will, neither."

"I don't know what you're referring to."

"Something like your refusal to forgive me, perhaps."

Susan stopped short in her tracks and turned to him, her eyes wide with astonishment.

"Forgive you?" she said. "Forgive you? I'm sorry, Henry, I feel as though I must have missed something. Have you asked me to forgive you? Have you so much as apologized?"

Again, he took a step back, his eyes filling with shame and the tacit acknowledgement that she was correct. But tacit wasn't enough. She put her hands on her hips and waited for him to speak.

"You're right," he said. "I haven't done what I ought to have done – because we've hardly had a chance to speak together since I realized you were here. And, I guess, for shame, too." He was quiet for a moment. "I still carry the guilt for what I did," he said. "Never fear."

Unexpectedly, Susan felt tears sparking behind her eyes.

"I don't want that," she said. "I'm not...I'm not vengeful, Henry."

"I know. You're a far better person than I am – and a far better woman than I ever deserved."

She wrung her hands, glancing up and down the street, and realized there were too many passersby who could observe their conversation. She hurried on, turning down a back alley to cut across to the house, and he followed her.

Out of sight of the town, she stopped again and turned to him, the words spilling from her lips.

"I don't want you to carry guilt, and I don't want you to apologize – I want you to explain yourself."

"Explain myself?"

"Seven years ago, you asked me to marry you. I had only one requirement – that you speak to my father. The next thing I know, you're on a train heading west, to marry someone else."

Henry shoved his hands in his pockets.

"I did speak to your father," he said. "And he told me he didn't think I was good enough for his daughter – his little girl, he said." His jaw clenched. "I don't think he meant it the way it sounded – maybe he said the wrong words, I don't know. But for a man who lived by his pride, it was too much to take. Without his blessing on our marriage, with his doubts about my fitness to be your husband, I felt I had no other choice but to leave."

Susan stared at him, wide-eyed.

"Why...why didn't you tell me?"

"He was your father." Henry shrugged. "I didn't want to destroy your relationship with him – I knew it was complicated as things were. I figured he'd tell you when he was ready, and you two could make up. If making up was needed – looking back on it now, I don't think he really intended to run me off. I think it was a test, a test of my loyalty and my love." He seemed to shrink into himself. "A test I failed."

Susan folded her arms. "Don't try to make me feel sorry for you…" Her voice wasn't as strong as she would have liked.

"I'm not. I promise, Susan, I'm not. I can't tell you how much I regretted what I'd decided to do – but it was too late to go back on my promise to Maria. And after I left, I knew that you wouldn't want me back anyhow." He heaved a sigh. "I thought of you almost every day – missing you and feeling guilty for it. Maria knew the truth, and she understood it. At least, she said she did, and I hope I didn't fail her as a husband, as Lucy's father…She was a sweet woman, Maria was. She deserved better than me, too."

Susan could hardly comprehend all he was saying. He gave her a look full of such longing and regret and shame, that her throat tightened and her eyes burned with tears.

"I can't tell you how sorry I am. So very, very sorry. I … well, I failed both you and me. And in a way, I also failed Maria. All I can do is ask for forgiveness." His voice was thick and rough and at that moment, she had never seen him look so vulnerable.

At long last, there it was, all out in the open. With a shock, Susan realized that despite her long-held bitterness toward Henry, he had been as honest as he had known how to be under the circumstances. More honest, more open than she was being herself, allowing the town to believe she was Zachariah Holden's widow. She half expected Henry to point this out, but he was evidently too much of a gentleman – more of a gentleman than she had ever expected.

The truth of it all was sinking in slowly. Her own father had been responsible for the sadness in her life, even as he had flung her singleness in her face over and over again in the years that ensued. Henry was likely right; Daniel Spencer probably hadn't intended to chase away his daughter's fiancé. But at the same time, years of bitterness and sorrow couldn't simply dissipate with a single explanation. And Henry should have been stronger, tougher, smarter than that.

Somehow, the explanation had only served to make her feelings even more confused than ever.

"I'm sorry for everything that has happened," she said. "But I really can't think about it now, Mr. Hudson. I'm far too busy."

He looked taken aback at the coldness in her tone but rallied all the same.

"Indeed," he said. "I'm sure that Mr. Wilson keeps you very busy."

His tone was immediately annoying.

"What do you mean by that?"

"You've only known him a few days, but I understand he's already squired you to supper at the inn."

"Squired?" she repeated, scoffing. "He knew I was spending all my evenings alone and invited me to dine with him. It was a very gentlemanly thing to do."

"I've invited you to dine with me, too," Henry pointed out, "but you've yet to even give me an answer."

"My dealings with Mr. Wilson are none of your concern."

"Is that so? Are you sure you didn't sit in the window of the inn hoping I might walk by and see you with another man?"

"Of all the outrageous claims."

"I knew it." He folded his arms and grinned at her. "You're trying to make me jealous."

"I…I'm not…how dare you."

"'How dare you' sounds like a very genteel thing to say, but it isn't exactly a denial, is it?" Henry pointed out.

Susan threw her hands up in the air. "I cannot speak to you when you're being like this," she said. "I can't speak to you at all. Good evening, Mr. Hudson."

She turned to go, and was arrested by the warm, gentle grip of his hand on her arm, turning her back to face him.

"Susan, wait. I'm sorry for teasing you – but I mean it, really. I mean it all." He took a deep breath, as though steeling himself to speak something very important. "When I saw you there in the tearoom, after all this time, I thought that God had at last heard my prayer. I've been wanting to make amends, to make up for how I hurt you – but I didn't know how. And now that I know your circumstances, and we're both here in Miles Gulch, I can't hide my feelings from you any longer – and there's no reason to. Susan, I love you as much now as I did the day we got engaged. I'll wait as long as it might take for you to forgive me. But please – please tell me that you'll give me another chance."

She stared at him, aghast, in shock, and unable to even formulate the words for an answer. How could he say this to her? How could he expect her to believe him?

And why was her treacherous heart suddenly singing with the knowledge of his confession?

At last, she managed to speak, but her words were empty and lacked conviction.

"I must go," she muttered. He let go of her arm, and she turned away from him, hurrying down the street, hurrying home, wondering whether the past ten minutes had really happened at all.

CHAPTER 9

The next morning did not bring any relief to her anxious mind. She arose early, when it was still dark, and made herself some coffee as she sat by the fire. It was the day before Christmas Eve, and she had no real plans for the holiday. Her dream of a happy, family Christmas was fading into the distance. For, of course, she couldn't take Lucy and Henry up on their offer now.

Though she still could hardly credit it for truly occurring, the memory of his voice, his words, his direct gaze continued to play through her mind over and over.

Henry Hudson still loved her.

He had never stopped loving her – even though he had left her and married another, even though he had let her father's careless words prevent them from being together. The last sad seven years of her life had been the result of one man's words and another man's actions, and she had borne the brunt of the consequences.

In her confused state, she wandered through the little house, picking up objects and setting them down again. Everything there had belonged to Zachariah Holden; she had no real ownership of them at all. When Ross Wilson moved in, she decided abruptly, she would leave everything but her clothing. She would start over, start anew.

Somewhere else…

But her heart shrank away from the idea of leaving Miles Gulch for good. As difficult as it would be to face the new year with Henry and Lucy living in the same town, as difficult as it would be to find somewhere else for her to stay, she could not turn her back on the town. She had grown attached to it, even in the short time she had lived there. She loved the people who came in for tea each day; she loved Mrs. Caroline and her polite, genteel ways. The only options were to go back to Boston – which she would not do – or to start over somewhere new all over again, and she simply did not want to.

And so, come what may, she would stay.

One thing was clear, however – she had to gently make it clear to Ross Wilson that she was not interested in his courtship. Though it shamed her to admit it, Henry had been right. Ross Wilson was a handsome, stalwart, kind, strong man, but she was as little interested in marrying him as she was in running away with Doctor Stevens. She had been using him to capture the attention of Henry Hudson, and that was all – and it wasn't fair to Ross.

She was pondering over how, exactly, to manage this in a way that would bring the least amount of pain to all involved when there was a ferocious pounding on the door below. Pulling her robe tightly over her nightdress, for she had not yet gotten dressed for the day, she padded down the stairs and pulled the door ajar. On the other side of it, Henry stood, hatless, his dark hair in a mess and his eyes wide. In the pale light of the pre-dawn, he looked like a homeless ghost.

"Susan, please – Lucy is sick."

Susan's heart stood still. "What's wrong?"

Henry wrung his hands. She opened the door and dragged him inside, realizing that he was out without a coat. Outside, the snow was beginning to fall, granting a silvery, ghostly light to the early day.

"What's wrong, Henry?"

"I don't know – a fever. She was tired yesterday, went to bed early and fell asleep. This morning I went to rouse her and she's not waking up. Susan…" His voice broke, and she saw the true extent of his worry. The memory flashed up to her – the knowledge that his wife, Maria, had died of a sudden illness. Mrs. Caroline's words, fearing that her mother's weak constitution had been passed down to Lucy, rang in her ears. "I went for the doctor, but Mrs. Stevens said he didn't come back last night. He was over in Millville, there's a bad case of the flu. Susan, I didn't know who else to go to…"

He stood with his head down, his eyes beseeching her, suddenly as innocent and helpless as a young boy. Susan reached out to put a hand in his tousled hair, unable to stop herself.

"I'll dress and come with you," she assured him. "I won't be a moment. Wait by the fire and warm yourself."

She fled up the stairs and dressed hastily, her numb fingers having trouble with the buttons. On a whim, she fetched Zachariah's coat from where it was neatly folded in the linen closet and took it down for Henry. Then back downstairs and collected him; he was still standing where she had left him, shivering.

She put a hand on his arm.

"I'll come now, Henry. Let's go."

He led her through the snowy streets, their hurried footsteps crunching on yesterday's frozen fall. Henry and Lucy lived not too far away from the mill itself where he worked; convenient for his employment, but a worrisome ways away from everything else. Susan didn't like to think of Lucy walking all this way by herself to reach the tearoom.

The little house was neat and tidy, with Lucy's drawings tacked up on every wall. Henry led Susan upstairs and stopped just outside the door.

"She's here."

Susan went in ahead of him and got to her knees beside the little cot. Lucy was asleep but murmuring in her uneasy dreams. Her forehead was hot as a firebrick and her clothing was damp with sweat. Susan couldn't chase away the memories of her own mother, falling ill in a similar manner – but her mother had been older, prone to sickness through her whole life. Lucy was younger, stronger, and she wasn't ready to let go of this life yet.

And neither her father nor Susan were ready to let go of her, either.

She stood up decisively, her hand still resting on Lucy's shoulder.

"Draw a bath of cold water," she directed. "We'll bring her fever down. When it's light, go back into town for Doctor Stevens, and leave word that he's to come here at once if he isn't home yet. Saddle your horse – we may need to move quickly."

Henry's eyes, full of love and pain, stared at her as though she were the only savior he'd ever known.

"Will she make it?" he asked hoarsely.

Susan squared her shoulders. She'd never felt so determined in her entire life. "She'll wake in time for Christmas," she said. "I promise."

"And you never break your promises," Henry said.

Susan faced him head-on. "I never do," she said.

CHAPTER 10

Somewhere in the early morning of Christmas Eve, Lucy awoke from her fever. Her eyelids fluttered, she stirred, and then her eyes opened fully to fix on Susan's joyous face.

"Susan?" she whispered. "Is it Christmas yet?"

Susan felt tears of joy spark behind her eyes, and she fell to her knees beside the bed and kissed the little girl on the forehead.

"Almost, but not quite," she told her. "Don't fall asleep again, dear, I'll go and fetch your father."

But Henry must have heard her voice, or perhaps that of his daughter, and when she stepped outside the room, he was there waiting. Their eyes met, and his contained a question – hers, an answer. She nodded, and he rushed into the room.

Susan stood at the doorway and looked in on them. Henry, the love of her life, so long away from her, on his knees beside his daughter. His handsome face was buried in the coverlet, and she knew he was praying with thanks for his daughter's preservation. As she watched, Lucy lifted a hand, trembling from her weakness, and laid it on her father's tumbled dark hair like a benediction.

Still fighting off tears, Susan turned and went back downstairs to make some tea.

The doctor had come and gone in the middle of the night, having finally arrived back to Miles Gulch from Millville. He had proclaimed Lucy to be on the mend and safe in Susan's capable hands and had gone off to much needed rest in his own bed. Still, even with his prediction of her recovery, it was much more thrilling to have Lucy awake and alert again. Though it might take some time, she would certainly be excited for Christmas Day the next morning.

Susan smiled to herself and turned from the tea things to find Henry standing in the doorway. They looked at each other for a moment, and then he crossed the kitchen in two long strides and took her into his arms. Susan rested her face against his chest, hearing the speedy beating of his heart, relishing the warmth and comfort of his arms around her. It had been a very long time since she had felt so safe and happy – seven years.

She felt his breath stir her hair as he spoke.

"You've kept your promise."

"I did. She's going to be just fine."

"Thank you, Susan – thank you for everything. And for… forgiving me."

She drew back and looked up at him.

"I didn't want to," she told him frankly. "In fact, I didn't intend to. But it happened without me even realizing it. I've spent so long mourning over your loss, Henry, that it was hard to let it go. But then I realized that you weren't lost at all – you never were. You're right here, with me."

"And I always have been," he whispered, and bent to kiss her.

She let him – she even kissed him back – but only for the briefest of times. Far too brief; he reached for her again when she stepped back, but she captured his hands and returned them to his sides.

"I must go," she said.

"Where to?"

"I have some explanations to make. I must tell Doctor Stevens that he was mistaken about his belief that I was married to Zachariah Holden – I must set the record straight and return the money for the blacksmith shop."

Henry shook his head. "There's no one to return it to," he said. "Zachariah had no family, and he was still pretty new here in town. If you don't have a claim on him, no one does."

"But that's just it – I don't have a claim on him."

"He agreed to marry you," Henry pointed out softly. "He would have done so. Not everyone breaks their promises like I do."

Susan shook her head.

"I still have no claim to his name," she said. "Whether they take the money or not, I'll leave up to the town. But as for the name of Mrs. Holden – I've got to go back to being Miss Spencer, and that's that."

Henry folded his arms and tilted his head. "Is that so?"

Something about the languid teasing in his voice stirred the butterflies in her stomach into flight. She dropped her gaze away from his.

"Yes. That's so."

"Suppose you took on yet another name – a legitimate one, this time."

Susan felt a smile tugging at the corners of her mouth. "What exactly are you proposing, Mr. Hudson?"

He stepped forward and put his hands on her waist, holding her still and looking down into her eyes.

"I'm proposing…" he said.

Susan caught her breath. "Yes?"

Henry Hudson threw back his head and laughed. "I'm proposing," he said. "And that's all."

Before she knew it, he was kissing her again, and this time she did not step back. At last, however, he drew back just a little, and smiled down at her.

"Now, if you insist on going to tell the truth to Doctor Stevens, why not wait for me to come with you? After all, with a fiancé there to protect you, even the terrible Doc Stevens won't be too upset."

"Oh, goodness, Henry. When have I ever needed anyone to protect me?"

"You've got a point," he acknowledged. His eyes softened to a fond shine as he looked at her, and he smoothed a hand over hair, placing another kiss on her forehead. "All right, then. Will you let me accompany you for my own peace of mind? Not that you need me – not that you need anyone. But I'd like to be there, by your side – where I should have been, these last seven years."

Susan Spencer smiled up at the man she was going to marry – at last.

"I suppose, when you put it like that…"

From the doorway, Lucy gave a little cry of delight. "It must be Christmas." she said. "Susan's here."

As she followed Henry over to wrap their arms around the little girl, Susan couldn't help but reflect on Lucy's words, and what they meant. They meant Susan's dream of a warm family Christmas would come true after all, and they meant Susan's long wait for love was over.

With her heart full of the warmth she'd been missing, Susan closed her eyes and smiled.

"Merry Christmas," she whispered.

The End

CONTINUE READING ...

Thank you for reading **Christmas Love Returns!** Are you wondering **what to read next?** Why not read **The Christmas Widow Bride? Here's a peek for you:**

The horse became aware of the disturbance before the noise reached Damon's ears. Instead of going easily into his stall, as the gelding always did at the end of a long day, his ears pricked forward, and he whickered softly, uneasily. Damon smoothed a hand over his glossy black neck, murmuring.

"What is it, Major?

But his favored horse would not be soothed. The animal backed nervously away from the stall, turning his head toward the direction of the barn doors – toward the ranch house.

That was when Damon heard the plaintive wail of his daughter.

With a prayer under his breath, he looped the reins around the gate of the stall and took off at a dead run toward the house. The screams were coming from the kitchen, and as he came through the front door, not stopping to kick his boots off as his mother always pleaded with him to do, they began to subside. By the time he reached the kitchen itself, Jessica was only giving an occasional cry, almost a keening, interspersed with whimpers. Damon's mother, eyes wide with fright, looked up at him. She was crouched on the floor, Jessica cradled in her arms. Near them, there was a pot upended on the ground, half the kitchen wet with the boiling water that must have spilled from it.

His three-year-old daughter looked up, her blue eyes wet with tears, and gave vent to a renewed crying. She stretched her arms out to him and he was horrified to see that one hand was violently red, the skin boiled and inflamed.

"Daddy. Daddy!"

"Damon, I warned her twice already – all I did was turn away for just a moment…"

"Shh, shh, now," Damon said, lifting Jessica into his arms. It was as much a soothing for his mother as it was for his daughter; it was obvious Sandra Osborne was in severe distress over what had happened to her only grandchild, and Damon knew his mother well enough to realize she would spend the next several months, if not years, guilting herself over providing inadequate care for Jessica. But it wasn't her fault – Sandra did her best with the child, but Jessica was born curious. She wasn't a troublemaker by nature, but her curiosity did lead her into scrapes – sometimes serious ones.

Smoothing one hand over Jessica's little shoulder, Damon coaxed her to turn her hand palm-up on his own so he could see the damage more clearly. He sucked in a breath through his teeth.

Visit HERE To Read More!
https://ticahousepublishing.com/mail-order-brides.html

THANKS FOR READING!

If you **love Mail Order Bride Romance**, <u>Visit Here</u>

https://wesrom.subscribemenow.com/

to find out about all <u>**New Susannah Calloway Romance**</u> <u>**Releases! We will let you know as soon as they become**</u> **available!**

If you enjoyed *Christmas Love Returns,* would you kindly take a couple minutes to leave a positive review on Amazon? It only takes a moment, and positive reviews truly make a difference. Thank you so much! I appreciate it!

Turn the page to discover more Mail Order Bride Romances just for you!

MORE MAIL ORDER BRIDE ROMANCES FOR YOU!

We love clean, sweet, adventurous Mail Order Bride Romances and have a lovely library of Susannah Calloway titles just for you!

Box Sets — A Wonderful Bargain for You!

https://ticahousepublishing.com/bargains-mob-box-sets.html

Or enjoy Susannah's single titles. You're sure to find many favorites! (Remember all of them can be downloaded FREE with Kindle Unlimited!)

Sweet Mail Order Bride Romances!

https://ticahousepublishing.com/mail-order-brides.html

ABOUT THE AUTHOR

Susannah has always been intrigued with the Western movement - prairie days, mail-order brides, the gold rush, frontier life! As a writer, she's excited to combine her love of story with her love of all that is Western. Presently, Susannah lives in Wyoming with her hubby and their three amazing children.

www.ticahousepublishing.com
contact@ticahousepublishing.com